Gateway from Hell

Lisa worked her way towards the front of the crowd. Luke was right up against the fence, yelling at the busy workers.

'Vandals! You're just vandals!'

Lisa tugged on his sleeve. He turned round.

'Just checking you're still here!'

Just then there was a gasp from the angry crowd, then wild cheering. Luke turned back to the fence, and stared, astonished.

The yellow digger had disappeared.

5

D0184227

Look out for other exciting stories
in the *Shades* series:

SHADES

Gateway from Hell

John Banks

Evans

Published by Evans Brothers Limited
2A Portman Mansions
Chiltern St
London W1U 6NR

© Evans Brothers Limited 2004

First published in 2004

British Library Cataloguing in Publication Data
Orme, David
Gateway From Hell. - (Shades)
1. Young adult fiction
I. Title
823.9'14 [J]

ISBN 0 237 52623 9

Series Editor: David Orme
Editor: Julia Moffatt
Designer: Rob Walster

Chapter One

The yellow digger bit deeply into the side of the hill. With a roar of its engine, it backed out and turned. It tipped a load of earth and stones into a waiting dumper truck.

A safe distance from the work was a high fence with barbed wire at the top. A crowd of people shouted and waved banners on the other side.

'Stop the road now! Don't murder the countryside!'

A row of policemen and security guards in yellow coats stood on the working side of the fence. More guards were waiting behind the protesters in case of trouble. They had worked on the site of the new bypass for months now. They knew that today would be the biggest protest yet. The machines were digging a cutting through Mott Hill. Mott Hill was a special place.

The shouting of the crowd grew louder and angrier as the digger cut a trench into the side of the hill. A bottle flew over the fence, followed by a stone. Police moved in. Big Jim, one of the leaders of the protest, pushed into the middle of the crowd.

'Keep it peaceful! Don't do anything stupid! You're just playing into their hands!'

Things were getting out of control. The

protestors were pushing on the fence, shaking it backwards and forwards. Another stone flew over. It bounced off the yellow plastic helmet of a security man. More police moved in. They started to make arrests.

Outside the fence, a radio journalist was busy finding people to interview. An elderly man tried to make himself heard over the noise. He was big and powerfully-built, with a bushy grey beard.

'Mott Hill has always been sacred land. Druids worshipped here. There was trouble before when this ground was disturbed!'

'But only a very small part of the hill is being lost, and the road will solve local traffic problems.'

'I've nothing against roads. But I tell you, digging here is dangerous.'

'Thank you for that.' The interviewer sounded as if he didn't believe him. 'This is Mike Short from the site of the Millchester bypass. Now, back to Jenny in the studio.'

With the arrest of the hotheads, the other protesters calmed down. One of them, a tall, dark-haired girl called Lisa, looked round anxiously. She sighed with relief. Luke, her boyfriend, was still there. He had been arrested before. He got very angry about the way the countryside was being destroyed.

She worked her way towards the front of the crowd. Luke was right up against the fence, yelling at the busy workers.

'Vandals! You're just vandals!'

Lisa tugged on his sleeve. He turned round.

'Just checking you're still here!'

Just then there was a gasp from the angry crowd, then wild cheering. Luke

8

turned back to the fence, and stared,
astonished.

The yellow digger had disappeared.

Chapter Two

Evening had come. The workers and most of the policemen had gone home. The protesters' camp was lit up with fires. It was early in the summer, and the nights were chilly. Lisa and Luke sat close to their fire, glad of the warmth. Lisa's dog, Raven, lay between them. Raven looked fierce and menacing, but he had never hurt anyone. He adored Lisa.

'It was incredible when the digger vanished down that hole,' said Lisa. 'I'm glad the driver wasn't hurt.'

'It would have served him right if he had been, if you ask me,' said Luke.

Lisa was more sympathetic. She knew that the driver of the digger was just an ordinary man, doing his job, even if they didn't agree with what he was doing. Luke always found it hard to control his anger. He had been through a lot in his life. He had never known his parents. He had spent his childhood running away from foster parents and children's homes. He had become very hard and bitter. He was never easy to get on with. Lisa was his first real friend.

They thought back to the amazing events of the morning. When the big digger moved further into the trench, the ground gave way. The machine slid head-first into a great hole in the hillside. The driver had managed to scramble out. A chain was fixed to the digger, and a giant dumper truck pulled it out.

Work had stopped for the day. Nothing could be done until the hole was filled in. Local archaeologists said that the hole had to be examined first, and that might take weeks. The road builders were not pleased.

Big Jim was listening to a radio. He shouted for people nearby to be quiet.

'They're doing something on the protest. Listen!'

They listened to a report of the day's events. They knew that radio and TV were important. A group of protestors couldn't beat the police and the road builders. They had to get their message across to the public.

The programme switched to an interview

with the man who had spoken on the radio that morning.

'Harold Dyson is a local expert on Mott Hill. He has strong views on the new road…'

'As I have said many times, digging up Mott Hill is dangerous! There is something there which must not be disturbed…'

Luke groaned.

'He's just a loony, that bloke!'

Lisa turned on him.

'Why can't you believe in something, Luke? There *is* something special about this hill. That's why we're here. Everyone can feel it, except you!'

Luke didn't believe in anything but his own anger. He was about to give one of his hard and bitter replies, but he didn't get the chance.

A terrible scream cut through the

dark night from the direction of the
road workings.

Chapter Three

There was a general rush towards the fence
to see what had happened. Jim told some of
the group to stay at the camp, in case it
was a trick by the security guards. They
might be planning to demolish the camp
while it was empty.

Down at the workings the floodlights
had been switched on. They looked

through the fence. They could see one man lying on the ground, and other figures in yellow jackets bending over him.

One of the men jumped up and came over to them. He was so angry he could hardly speak.

'Which one of you worthless scum did this then? There's a good man there, dead! By God, when I find out…'

Big Jim tried to calm him down.

'Look, mate, we don't go round killing people, yeah? Whatever happened to that guy, it wasn't us.'

The security guard wouldn't listen. He carried on raving.

'He was a good mate of mine. He had a wife, and young kids. The whole lot of you should be strung up and burnt…'

For once, the protesters were glad there was a fence.

Blue lights flashed up the trackway to the site – an ambulance and police cars.

'Let's get back to the camp,' said Jim. 'The old bill have arrived, and there's going to be big trouble.'

The trouble came about fifteen minutes later, when the police stormed into the camp. A chief inspector, in his smart uniform, stood in the centre. He spoke into a megaphone.

'A man has been killed tonight. Everyone here is under suspicion. No one will leave until they have been interviewed.'

Another policeman walked into the camp. He spoke urgently to the chief inspector, who nodded and barked out orders. They started searching the tents and rough shacks, flashing torches into every dark corner. They ignored the complaints of the protestors who had started settling down for the night.

They shone a torch into Luke and Lisa's tent. Raven growled threateningly.

'Over here, sir.'

The chief inspector ordered them out of the tent.

'Is this your dog? It looks like a dangerous animal to me.'

'Raven? He wouldn't hurt anybody.'

'Really? That man's throat was torn out by a large animal. Constable, get the dog-handler up here and collect that dog.'

'Leave him alone! I've told you, he wouldn't hurt anybody!'

But the police wouldn't listen. The dog-handler fixed a muzzle over Raven's mouth, and bundled him into a van.

Chapter Four

Lisa spent the night in tears. Luke tried to
cheer her up. The trouble was, he wasn't
very good at that sort of thing. He could
handle policemen, but dealing with his
friends was much more difficult. He had
had a tough life and it had made him hard.
He found it difficult to trust anyone, even
Lisa. No one had ever loved him, or even

liked him much. People had always let him down. Maybe even Lisa would let him down in the end.

Next morning Lisa was woken up by the sound of barking. Raven was back.

At first she thought he must have escaped, but a policeman was standing outside her tent with him on a lead.

'He's in the clear. Forensic say the teeth marks on the dead man don't match your dog. They don't think it was a dog at all. And we've had some more incidents. They happened when your dog was locked up – so it can't have been him.'

He looked at Lisa.

'You seem like a nice girl. How come you've got mixed up with all these dropouts? Haven't you got a home to go to?'

Lisa saw red.

'I'm not a nice girl, they're not dropouts,

and I don't have to listen to lectures!'

The policeman held up his hands.

'OK, OK! Just take my advice, and…'

Lisa smiled sweetly at him.

'And whatever you say, I'll do the complete opposite.'

Lisa was happy to have Raven back, but everyone else in the camp was in a gloomy mood. Protests were one thing. A savage death was quite another. The police would get really heavy now.

Later on, a Land Rover pulled up in the camp. Two men got out. One of them was carrying a shotgun. They looked angry.

'Where's that dog then?' said one of them. 'I've got three sheep with their throats ripped out. If the police won't deal with it, we will.'

Raven was lying in the sunshine, recovering from his fright of the night

21

before. One of the farmers spotted him.

'There he is, Jack. Get him, quick.'

With a scream Lisa jumped up and threw herself on top of the surprised Raven. The farmer tried to pull her off. Other people joined in, fighting with both of them.

The police had been expecting trouble. Half-a-dozen officers burst into the clearing, and the brawl came to an end. Luke had been in the thick of the fighting. Two policemen were holding him back.

'Come to help your friends, then?' said Luke, taunting one of the policemen, who said, 'When will you learn that we're here to protect you, just like everyone else!'

He turned to the two farmers.

'I'm placing you two under arrest for a firearms offence.'

They got angry.

'We've got a right to shoot dogs that worry sheep.'

'Not here you haven't, with people around. Constable, take that gun away from them. As for the rest of you, take my advice and clear out of here. There's something very nasty about. We don't know what it is, but it's a lot bigger than a dog and much more dangerous. I don't want any more dead bodies to deal with!'

Chapter Five

After the police had left, the protest group
talked about what they should do next.
Some people didn't believe the story. They
thought it was just a trick to get rid of
them. Others were frightened.

The camp and the roadworks were full of
journalists. One of them was Mike Short,
the local radio journalist. The members of

the group trusted him. He had always been fair. They asked him about the story.

'Yes, it's true. I've seen the sheep myself. They were in a terrible mess. One of them was completely ripped apart.'

Lisa was thinking about the radio interview. She couldn't get it out of her mind.

'*Mott Hill is dangerous! There is something there that shouldn't be disturbed…*'

'That man you interviewed. Where could I find him?'

'Harold Dyson? He's an odd bloke! He lives over the hill in Chapelbrook, by the post office.'

Luke looked at Lisa.

'You mean the nutter?' he sneered. 'Don't make me laugh!'

Lisa could get angry too. Too furious for words, she went into the tent and gathered up her few belongings. Luke tried to stop her.

'Lisa, I'm sorry. I didn't mean…'

But Lisa stormed out of the camp, taking Raven with her.

Harold Dyson was easy to find. He was sitting in his garden, looking through some old books. His big body and tangled beard made him look frightening. When he heard why Lisa had come, he welcomed her. He rushed off to make some tea.

'It isn't the first time this has happened,' he said. 'I've been going through the records. The last time was in 1698. People were digging chalk out of Mott Hill, and the big hole was uncovered. Three people died then, and many animals. It only stopped when the hole was filled in again.'

'But what are they?'

'I don't know what they look like. The

old records talk about demons. Some people think that Mott Hill is man-made. They say it was put there to stop these things escaping.'

'But why don't you tell someone?'

'I have told them. And what do they say? "Harold Dyson, the village lunatic. It's just an animal escaped from the zoo."'

He snorted. 'There isn't a zoo for miles around!'

'What can we do then?'

'Close up the gateway!'

'What do you mean, the gateway?'

'That hole in the hill. Lisa, I'm not a religious person, but sometimes I wonder if it isn't a gateway straight from hell!'

Chapter Six

Late that afternoon they set off back to the camp. On the way it started to rain. By the time they got to the camp there was a steady drizzle.

There was great activity at the camp. The protest group had decided to move into the trees.

'There's no way we're moving out,' said

Big Jim. 'But if there is something prowling about, we'll be safer sleeping on our tree platforms.'

Lisa introduced Harold to the group. Luke was looking sulky, so Lisa ignored him. Luckily they hadn't taken down the tents yet. They crowded into the largest one to hear what Harold had to say. They didn't all fit in. Some people listened from outside, holding plastic sheets over their heads.

Harold told them what he had told Lisa.

'What happened in 1698 is happening again. You can hide in the trees if you like. But there is no escape from them.'

There was silence for a moment. Then Ed, one of the tree platform builders, spoke.

'It's going to be a big job, filling that hole. You need machinery for that.'

Then Luke spoke.

'Not a problem. I can operate one of those

diggers. I had a go in one on the last protest, and I don't need keys to start one up.'

Some of Luke's friends laughed. They remembered where that digger had ended up. Luke was lucky not to have been caught.

'What about the security guards and the police?'

'They've gone. Scared of being eaten by wild animals!'

Lisa went over to Luke. 'I thought you didn't believe in all this?' she said.

'I don't. I just like driving diggers!'

Harold was invited to stay in the camp until dark. Then the raid would take place. Pete would cut a hole through the wire, then Jim, Luke, Lisa and Harold would go through. Luke would operate the digger while the others would try to light up the scene with torches.

The rain fell steadily all afternoon and

evening. The group tried to keep dry.
At last the 'task force' (as they called
themselves) got ready to go. Lisa insisted
that Raven came with them. She wouldn't
let him out of her sight.

Luke heard a noise outside when he was
putting on an extra waterproof.

'Shut up you lot.'

They heard a strange snuffling
noise, mixed in with hisses and grunts.
Something was heading up the path
from the fence.

'Into the trees!'

There was a scramble to climb up into
the trees. Raven had to be lifted up. They
thought that Harold would need help, but
he was very fit for his age.

Something was in the camp below. Lisa
and Luke could hear it under their tree. It
seemed to know they were there. It circled

round, hissing and spitting. Raven was terrified. Lisa could feel the animal's heart beating fast as she held him.

With a great snarl the beast leapt up at the tree. They heard huge claws scraping at the bark. The whole tree shook.

The creature realised it couldn't reach them. It snarled once more, then set off to look for easier prey.

'Quick,' said Harold. 'While it's away, we can deal with the hole. Let's get moving!'

Chapter Seven

The rain still poured down. Pete went first, with the wire cutters. There were no security men to stop him so he soon made a large hole in the fence.

'Look at that!'

Big Jim had noticed a hole right by the fence. Whatever the beast was, it had dug its way under. Harold examined it carefully by torchlight.

'It's huge,' he said. 'And look at those claw marks on the ground!'

The task force slipped into the work site. Diggers and dumper trucks stood abandoned in the darkness. Luke went over to the nearest digger. The rest went and shone torches down the hole.

'Phew, what a stink!'

A terrible smell came up from the hole. There were more claw marks there, easy to see in the muddy ground.

Lisa had a sudden thought.

'Harold, we can't fill it in now. The creature is still outside. We need to wait until it comes back.'

Harold shook his head.

'No, Fill it in! Trap the creature here. We'll have to deal with it later.'

Big Jim wasn't sure.

What are we dealing with, anyway?' he said. 'I'm beginning to get a bad feeling about the whole business.'

Then they heard Luke calling. He came over with bad news.

'I can't start the digger,' he said. 'They've fitted some new security device. The engine is immobilised.'

'Right,' said Jim. 'Pete, go and get everyone down here. There are shovels about, and pick-axes. We'll use our bare hands if we have to. We'll get this hole filled before that thing gets back.'

'I'm on my way,' said Pete, disappearing into the darkness.

The rest of the task force turned off their torches to save the batteries. It was frightening, standing there in the dark, knowing that the creature could return at any moment.

Luke thought he heard a sound coming from the hole. They all listened carefully, but heard nothing.

'Probably just a loose stone rolling down,' said Harold. 'But look. Can you see anything down there?'

They all looked. Their eyes were used to the dark by now. At the bottom of the hole they could see a faint light.

'Listen,' said Luke. 'There's that sound again!'

They all heard it this time. A hissing and scrabbling was coming from the hole, getting louder all the time.

Another creature was coming through the gateway.

Chapter Eight

The creature was on them before they had a chance to run. They could make out a shape in the dark. It walked on two legs, and was as tall as a human being. A terrible smell came from its body. Huge arms hung down by its side.

They all tried to turn and run towards the hole in the fence but it was hard going over the soft, sticky ground.

The creature snarled in anger. Its arm struck out at Luke, and he felt a blow on the side of the head. Luckily, it had hit him with the back of its hand, not its claws.

Suddenly Pete arrived with everyone from the camp. They carried torches and shone them on the creature from the other side of the fence.

At last they could see it. It was dark brown and scaly, with a face like a wolf. Its eyes were huge. White slime trailed from its jaws. A tail dragged along the ground. If there was such a place as hell, surely this creature must have come from it.

The creature seemed to hate the light. It covered its dazzled eyes with its arms.

Lisa could feel herself slipping in the mud. The creature was right behind her. She felt a terrible pain as one claw of its foot scratched her shoulder through her coat as she sprawled on the ground.

At that moment, Raven leapt for it. He had seen it attack his beloved Lisa. He sank his teeth into its scaly leg.

The dazzled creature couldn't see what was hurting it. It let out a dreadful shrieking howl. From behind the people by the fence came an answering howl. The other creature had come back.

There was instant panic. Everyone was desperate to escape. Running this way and that, they stumbled off through the woods, taking their torches with them.

Now the creature could see again. Frightened by the savage nip from Raven, it rushed towards the tunnel under the fence. Raven chased it, barking madly. Lisa managed to scramble up again.

'Raven! Come back!'

The creature coming down the path was much braver than the one that had hurt Lisa. It forced its way through the hole cut in the fence.

Harold was still standing near the hole. The new creature decided to make him a target. Harold cried out in alarm. He could only just make out the creature's shape in the dark, but he knew that the wicked claws were coming towards his face.

Suddenly there was the roar of an engine. The generator! The floodlights flickered and came on. The whole scene was as bright as day. The creature screamed and put its paws over its eyes. With a huge leap, it reached the pit and slithered down inside.

Harold was dazzled too. He took a step back and slipped on the wet mud. He started to slide feet first down the hole.

There was nothing to hold onto to stop him falling. Lisa was the nearest. She threw herself down on the ground and grabbed his hands just as they disappeared over the edge of the hole.

Harold was too heavy for her, but she wouldn't let go until she felt herself sliding down as well. When she did let go, it was too late. She was sliding head-first down the hole, with no idea how deep it was, or what was at the bottom.

Chapter Nine

The site engineer did not believe a word of the fantastic story. He had heard the noise from the site office down the hill and had turned on the lights. When he got up the hill, the action was all over.

'Monsters from hell? Do you expect me to believe that? I believe what I see with my own eyes. Serious damage to a fence.'

He looked at the digger.

'Someone's tried to force their way in here, too.'

He talked into a small radio.

'Ted? Bring the lads up here, will you? More trouble. And ring the police.'

For the first time in years, Luke's hard shell broke down. He was in tears.

'Look, I'm telling you, my girlfriend's fallen down that hole. She might be hurt. She needs help.'

The site engineer sighed.

'This had better be true. I know you lot. You'd do anything to cause trouble.'

Big Jim came over.

'Look, I didn't see it, but if Luke says that's what happened, that's what happened.'

Ted and four security men arrived in a Land Rover. It had a winch at the front.

One of the men agreed to go down the hole on a rope.

Ted started the engine on the winch and the man was slowly lowered down. He had taken another small rope to signal with.

Ted held the other end of the rope. Two tugs. That meant the man had reached the bottom. Three tugs. Haul him up.

The man was winched out of the hole. He was covered in mud from head to foot.

'Nothing down there at all, except mud,' he said.

Luke couldn't believe it. The lights had been on. He had seen them go sliding down with his own eyes.

'They must be there. You can't have looked properly. Let me go down!'

'Oh yes, and then refuse to come up again! That's your game, is it? I'm not falling for that one.'

What happened next shouldn't have happened. Lisa was gone. Lisa. The only person that Luke had ever cared about, even if he hadn't been able to say so properly. And here was a bloke with a sneering face calling him a liar.

He thumped him. Hard. Two of Ted's men grabbed him and pulled him back. If the police hadn't arrived back at that moment, Luke might have got a few thumps in return.

Luke tried to calm down and explain what had happened. That would be the best thing for Lisa. But the police didn't believe him either. Even Big Jim was beginning to doubt him.

'Are you sure, Luke? They said they weren't down there. Even this lot wouldn't just leave them there.'

A policeman went and peered in the hole.

'You'd better have another look
down there in the morning, just to be sure,'
he said.

The engineer was not in the mood to
agree to anything.

'All right,' he said. 'But it'll have to be
early. Those archaeologists have decided
that they're not interested in the hole after
all. I've got two lorryloads of hardcore to
tip down it. I wish all you lot were down at
the bottom when I do.'

Chapter Ten

Lisa was badly bruised when she got to the bottom of the hole. She had slid all the way down, and sharp stones had cut into her clothes.

She landed with a thump. For a minute she did not move or open her eyes. When she did, she saw a faint light. It shone up from a square patch on the floor of the hole. She looked around for Harold, but there was no sign of him. He must have tumbled down further, through the square opening.

She shuddered. She didn't want to go through that hole. But Harold might need her help.

She crept over to the square hole and looked down. She could see a rocky tunnel below. The walls shone with a strange green light. By this light, she could see Harold lying on the ground.

'Here goes!' she said, and slipped through the tunnel feet first.

It was an odd feeling, jumping down into the tunnel. She felt dizzy and sick for a few seconds.

She tried very hard not to land on Harold. She hoped he hadn't hurt himself too badly. It would be very difficult getting such a big man out again.

As she reached Harold, he groaned and sat up.

'Are you all right, Mr Dyson?'

'I think so. I'm getting a bit old for this at my age. I'm very bruised, but nothing is broken, thank goodness.'

That was a relief. Lisa tried to help Harold get up. It was a low tunnel, and he couldn't stand upright.

'How are we going to get out of here?' said Lisa.

'Up the way we came. Through the square hole.'

But when they looked up, the hole had disappeared. They could see nothing but a rocky ceiling. Harold banged on it, but everything seemed solid.

'We'd better see where the tunnel leads,' he said.

They set off along the tunnel. Before they left the place, Harold wedged a piece of paper between two stones in the wall.

'Just so we know where the gateway was,' he said.

After a few paces, the tunnel turned and stopped. A solid wall faced them.

'We'd better try the other way,' said Harold.

They turned and walked back. When they reached the piece of paper, they looked up hopefully. Had the gateway come back? The roof was as solid as ever.

Harold was finding it difficult to walk. He had to stoop, which made his back ache. What was worse, they could smell the horrible stink of the scaly creatures. They must have passed that way.

The tunnel opening came quite suddenly. It was dark outside. Harold and Lisa pushed through bushes. They found themselves on the side of a hill. There was no rain, and, strangely, the ground seemed quite dry. Stars shone through gaps in patchy clouds. There was a strange scent in the air. It wasn't horrible like the creatures, but Lisa couldn't tell what it was.

By the faint starlight, they could see down into a wide valley. It was quiet. All they could hear was the wind rustling through the bushes. It didn't look anything like hell.

Suddenly Harold grabbed Lisa by the arm. He pointed upwards.

'Look!' he said, in a shaking voice.

Lisa looked up. The clouds had moved over, leaving a large gap. Moonlight shone through it, lighting up the valley.

Lisa gasped.

There were two moons in the sky.

Chapter Eleven

The clouds were clearing now, and Harold and Lisa could see more and more of the sky. The stars shone down brightly. They seemed brighter than Lisa had ever seen them before.

'Where on earth are we?'

'That's just it. I don't think we *are* on Earth. Look at those moons, and the stars!'

'You mean … we're on Mars, or somewhere? That's just stupid!'

'Not Mars. Much further away than that. The moons are too big. In any case, the star patterns would look the same from Mars.'

At one end of the valley, the sky seemed lighter. Morning was coming! Minute by minute, they could see more clearly.

'How can it be? How can we possibly travel millions and millions of miles just by jumping through a hole?'

Harold shook his head. 'I've no idea about that. One thing I am sure of; those creatures must live here. Perhaps they passed through the gateway by mistake, just like we did.'

Lisa nodded slowly. 'Perhaps that's how people used to travel through space. Through gateways that bend space round so you can travel anywhere in seconds. I saw a science fiction film once where people could do that. Maybe the gateway on Earth has been forgotten and covered up for years and years.'

The sun came up. It seemed much bigger and brighter than the sun they were used to.

'I can't understand why the creatures hated the light,' said Lisa. 'You'd need sunglasses to live here.'

'I'd guess they live underground, and only come out at night to hunt,' said Harold. 'With their big eyes, the moonlight and starlight would be very bright to them.'

They could see right across the valley now. Tall, thin trees were scattered here and there. They had long, dark green leaves, and did not look like Earth trees at all. Across the valley, they could see an enormous pile of stones. It looked like the remains of a ruined castle. At the bottom of the valley there was a stream. A road ran along the side of it.

'Look at that,' said Harold. 'A road. That must mean people.'

'How do you know they will be people?' said Lisa. 'They might be anything. And they might be very unfriendly.'

'Listen!' said Harold. 'What's that sound?'

Figures appeared at the far end of the valley. It looked as if something was being slowly dragged along. Now and then they could hear shouts, and a cracking sound.

'I think now would be a good time to hide,' said Harold.

They hid behind the bushes and watched. The figures looked quite human. A group of them, men and women, were dragging a huge cart. Another group sat in the wagon. They were dressed in a blue uniform. Now and then one of them yelled and cracked a whip at the people dragging the heavy cart. Apart from the people in blue, the cart was loaded with boxes and what looked like bales of cloth.

'Slaves!' whispered Harold. 'Not friendly then. We'd better keep very quiet.'

Lisa was crouched in an uncomfortable position. She moved her feet and stepped on a loose stone. What was worse, she lost her balance and found herself sliding down the hillside!

A cry went up from below. The men in blue took long weapons from their shoulders and pointed them at Lisa. Two of them started to run up the hill towards her.

'Quick!' shouted Harold. 'Back into the tunnel!'

As soon as they started to run for the tunnel, the men below fired their weapons. Luckily, they weren't very accurate. With bullets hitting the ground around them, Harold and Lisa reached the tunnel and scrambled inside.

'Come on,' said Harold. 'Maybe the gateway has opened again.'

They set off down the tunnel. About half way to the gateway, they stopped to listen. They heard shouting from behind them. The blue soldiers were coming down the tunnel!

Then they heard another sound. A hissing and scraping sound. Ahead of them. The gateway was open again, and the other creature had returned.

Chapter Twelve

'Quick,' said Harold. 'See if your torch is still working!'

Lisa switched her torch on. Nothing happened. She gave it a bang and the light shone out. Harold's torch was working too.

They moved on down the passage. The gateway was open again, and the creature crouched right underneath it.

It didn't seem to know which way to go.

'Shine your torch!' said Harold. 'Drive it along to the dead end!'

The scaly creature squealed at the bright light and scuttled along the tunnel. The smell was terrible in that small space.

'Now, quick,' said Harold. 'Up you get!'

Lisa scrambled up through the opening. As she passed through, she felt dizzy and sick again. She turned to help Harold through. He found the climb difficult, but at last he managed it. Puffing, they sat at the bottom of the hole in a huge puddle. Above them, it was still night, but the rain had stopped.

Below, in the tunnel, they could hear muffled shouts. Then suddenly, they stopped. The glowing light was gone.

The gateway was closed once more.

It was impossible to climb out of the

deep, slippery hole. It was a long wait for daylight in the cold. At last, a grey light started to seep down. They tried yelling for help, but there was no one to hear them.

At last, they heard noise from above. The roaring of machinery. Shouts and yells. Earth and small stones started to fall in on them. A bigger stone hit Lisa on the shoulder. Suddenly there were loud yells, and a scrabbling sound. Something was coming down the hole. Surely there wasn't another creature on the loose?

It landed in a flurry of paws and a frantically-licking tongue.

'Raven,' cried Lisa. 'Oh, you lovely dog!'

It had been a close thing. The dumper trucks had just started to tip their loads down the hole when Raven had rushed through the security men and jumped down it. Somehow, he had known Lisa was down there. The tipping had been stopped and a man was sent down to rescue the dog. He was astonished to find two people there too.

Harold and Lisa were rushed to hospital, but they only had cuts and bruises. Lisa had a nasty scratch on her shoulder from the creature. Mike Short, from the radio station, wanted to hear their story, but Harold said that it would be better not to say too much. Lisa agreed. Who would believe them anyway?

She didn't think that Luke would believe a word of it. After hitting the engineer he had been taken to the police station to cool off in a cell. When the news came through that Lisa and Harold had been found down the hole, he was released without charge.

When Lisa had finished telling Luke her story, she looked at him.

'I don't suppose you believe a word of it, do you?'

Luke thought about it for a minute.

'That's always been my problem, hasn't it? I've never believed in anything, not even myself. Lisa, I was terrified when they couldn't find you down that hole. Then I was locked up so I couldn't find you myself. I knew that the hole was going to be filled in. I thought I would never see you again. Now I've got you back. That's a miracle. It looks as though I'm going to have to start believing in miracles!'

Down below, the roar of machinery had started again. The tent flap was pushed aside and Big Jim looked in.

'Work's started again. They'll be able to start building the road now that they've filled in the hole. Come on you two. No slacking. We've got some serious protesting to do!'